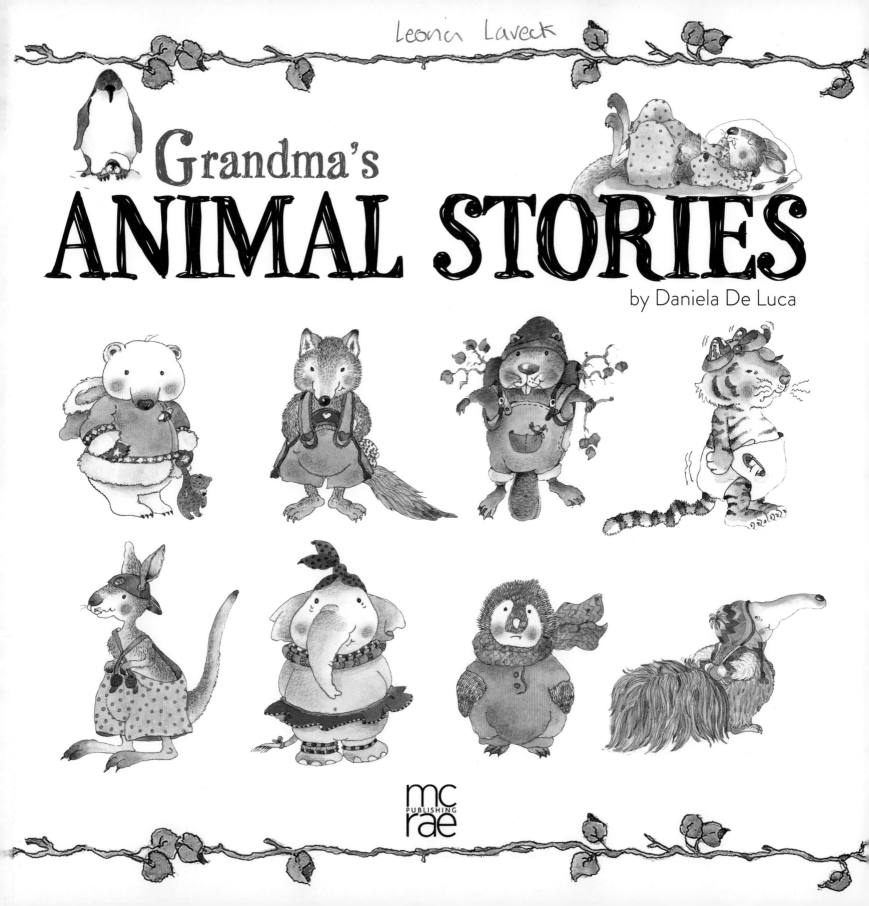

Leonia Laveck

Grandma's
ANIMAL STORIES

by Daniela De Luca

mc
rae
PUBLISHING

All illustrations by Daniela De Luca
Texts: Daniela De Luca, Anne McRae, Neil Morris
Editing: Anne McRae, Vicky Egan, Neil Morris
Graphic Design: Marco Nardi
Layout: Marco Nardi, Rebecca Milner

ISBN 978-1-910122-10-5

2 4 6 8 10 9 7 5 3 1

Repro: Litocolor, Florence, Italy
Printed and bound in China

Contents

4   Introduction

7   Mattie the Polar Bear

37   Ben the Beaver

67   Harry the Wolf

97   Celia the Tiger ✓

127   Josh the Anteater ✓

157   Lizzie the Elephant

187   Buster the Kangaroo

217   Bob the Penguin

246   Quiz

Introduction

THE EIGHT STORIES in this book cover a whole world of animals. In each story we follow a typical animal from one region and meet many other animals that share the same environment. The main characters are based on real animals, but the stories are imaginary. As you read their adventures, you will find information boxes and fun facts telling you all about real animals' lives.

IN THE STORIES you will meet a polar bear from the Arctic region, a beaver from North America, a wolf from Europe, a tiger from the Asian country of India, an anteater from South America, an elephant from Africa, a kangaroo from the Australian bush, and a penguin from frozen Antarctica. The maps show where these continents are in the world.

ARCTIC

ARCTIC REGION

Mattie the Polar Bear

AFRICA

Lizzie the Elephant

NORTH AMERICA

Ben the Beaver

SOUTH AMERICA

Josh the Anteater

ASIA

Celia the Tiger

EUROPE

Harry the Wolf

AUSTRALIA

Buster the Kangaroo

ANTARCTICA

Bob the Penguin

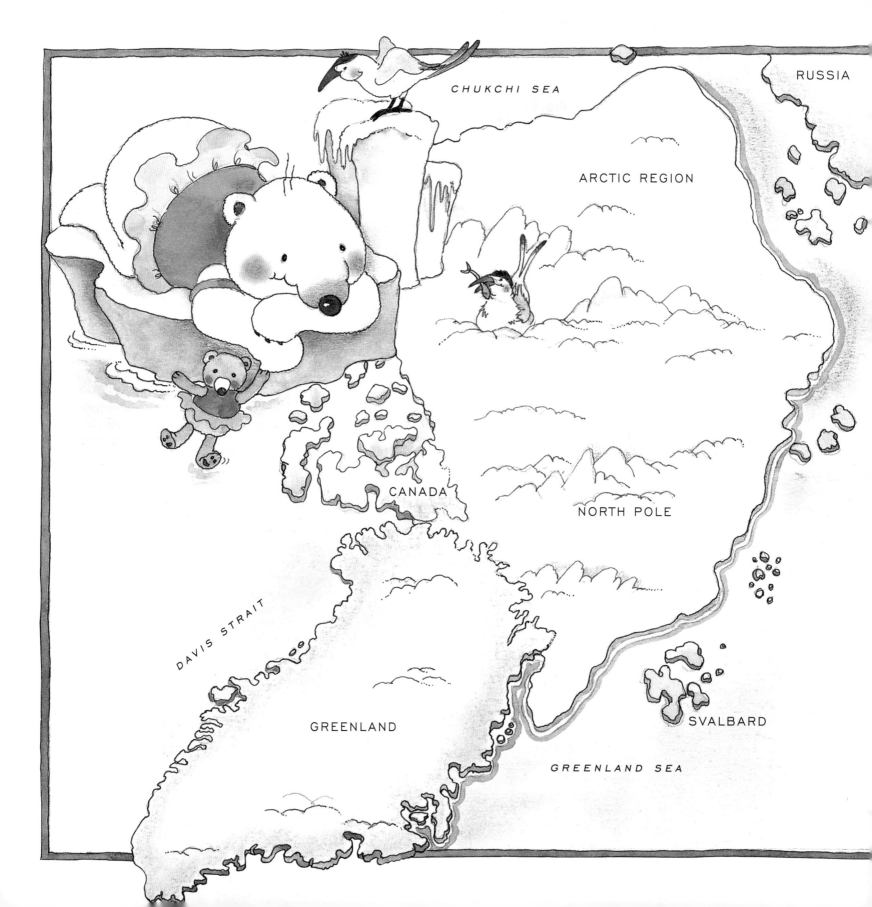

RUSSIA

CHUKCHI SEA

ARCTIC REGION

CANADA

NORTH POLE

DAVIS STRAIT

GREENLAND

SVALBARD

GREENLAND SEA

Mattie
the Polar Bear

DO POLAR BEARS SLEEP ALL WINTER?
Adult females sleep in winter when they are expecting babies. They dig a den in a snowdrift, sleep there most of the time, and then give birth to their cubs. The cosy den is a safe and warm home for the tiny bears. Male polar bears are active all year round.

MOTHER POLAR BEAR WAKES UP with a start. She has had a very long sleep and wonders what day or even month it is. "Well, it's certainly gone 9 o'clock, and little Mattie will want her breakfast," she thinks. But her cub is still fast asleep. "I'd better check if we've got any food left. I haven't been out all winter," Mother growls to herself.

HOME
SWEET
HOME

9

WHILE THE BEARS WERE ASLEEP in their den, spring has come to Arctic Island. Mrs. Ermine is taking her children for a walk in the snow. "Don't play around the polar bear's den," she warns them. But cheeky Ernie shows off his new sledging skills when his mother's not looking.

ARE ALL POLAR BEAR DENS THE SAME?

They vary in shape and size, and they even change as wind blows fresh snow over the top. In very windy places, there may be a mound of snow over the entrance to the den.

Polar bears live in the Arctic region.
This is the area of frozen sea around
the North Pole. The bears live mainly
at the edge of the pack ice.

Oh dear, there's nothing in the den to eat, only
a few old fish bones. "That won't be enough
to feed a growing cub," says Mother Bear.
Just then Mattie wakes up. "I'm starving,"
she yawns. "What's for breakfast?"

RINGED
SEALS

EGGS

BIRD

KELP

WHAT DO POLAR BEARS EAT?
Tiny cubs feed off their mother's milk. When
they are older, polar bears' main food is ringed
seal. They also hunt lemmings, voles, and small
birds, as well as walrus pups.

VOLE

LEMMING

WALRUS PUP

12

ARE POLAR BEAR CUBS REALLY TINY?

Yes, they are much smaller than other animals when compared to the size of their mother. Cubs are born blind and deaf, and they have very thin fur. Their mother keeps them warm.

DO POLAR BEAR MOTHERS HAVE TWINS?

Yes, in fact about three quarters of births are of twins. Some mothers have a single cub, and occasionally they have triplets.

MOTHER BEAR TELLS MATTIE that they have to go to Wally Walrus's store to buy food. "We'd better wrap up warm," she says, zipping up the cub's jacket.

BEFORE THEY SET OFF, Mother has a quick look in the mirror. She's pleased with her new green coat. When they make their way across the ice, it creaks under their paws.

WHY DON'T POLAR BEARS SLIP ON THE ICE?
Because their big paws act like snowshoes. They have short, sharp claws with fur padding, which give them a good grip on ice and snow.

WALLY WALRUS IS BUSY TODAY. He's in a very good mood, handing out candy and telling everyone proudly that he has just become a father. "Could we see the little pup?" Mother Bear asks politely. "Of course!" Wally says.

They are not the only visitors.
Mrs. Seal has come with her daughter
Sissy to show her own new pup.

Mother Bear congratulates the other mothers, and then they
catch up on the island gossip. Mattie and Sissy soon get bored.
"Let's have a play in the snow," Mattie whispers, and the two
youngsters quietly sneak out of the room.

ARE POLAR BEARS GOOD SWIMMERS?

Yes, adults are very strong swimmers and can cover long distances without resting. Their small head and long neck give them a streamlined shape. They can also swim underwater for up to two minutes.

HOW DO POLAR BEARS GET DRY?

After swimming, they shake themselves and their thick fur throws the water off.

OUT ON THE ICE, Mattie tells Sissy that she is learning ballet. "I'll show you," she says, taking off her jacket. To Sissy's surprise Mattie is all dressed up, ready to dance. In her pink leotard she looks like a real ballerina.

MATTIE DOES A ROLY-POLY arabesque, a pretty
pirouette, and some jeté jumps. She glides
along on tiptoe, when suddenly there is a
loud cracking noise. A block of ice breaks
away and takes Mattie with it.
"Oh, no!" Sissy squeals.

19

WHAT IS AN ICEBERG?

Icebergs are huge chunks of ice that
break off from glaciers and ice shelves.
They float away, and only the top part
shows above the water. Most of the
iceberg is under the surface.

WHITE WHALE

MATTIE FLOATS AWAY on the ice and is soon out of sight.
Her mother is horrified when she sees what
has happened. "Oh dear, I don't know who
can save her now," says Grandma Arctic Hare.
"Oh dear, neither do I," says Grandpa Hare.

THE HOODED SEALS try to help, but all they can save is Mattie's teddy bear. Mattie grabs it and floats on. "Too much dancing," says Mr. Arctic Wolf. "Too near the edge," says Mrs. Arctic Fox. "What drama!" screech the terns as they fly overhead.

WHAT ARE THE DANGERS FOR CUBS?

A fall on the ice might injure a polar bear cub. If it breaks a bone, it might not be able to keep up with its mother. It needs to stay close, because adult male bears sometimes kill cubs.

24

THE PUFFINS CAN SEE that Mattie is now in real danger.
A gigantic, growling polar bear rears up on his hind legs
and lifts a powerful paw. He looks ready to swallow
Mattie and her teddy in a single mouthful.

LUCKILY THE STRONG OCEAN CURRENT floats Mattie out of reach of the huge growling bear. But before she knows it, she crashes into a big gray mountain rising up out of the sea. "Maybe it's a new Arctic island," Mattie thinks.

DO POLAR BEARS REALLY TRAVEL ON ICE FLOES?

Yes, in the summer adult polar bears follow the shifting pack ice as it melts into floes, or sheets of floating ice. Sometimes blocks of ice break away, so females keep an eye on their cubs and keep them close.

"THIS ISLAND IS VERY SOFT," Mattie thinks, "and very slippery too!" She just manages to cling on to the moving island.

BUT IT'S NOT AN ISLAND AT ALL! Lucky Mattie sees that she has been rescued by an old friend of her mother's. She's a helpful whale and she knows these waters well. "You can call me Auntie Wendy," she tells Mattie. "Now, let's get you home."

MOTHER BEAR AND HER FRIENDS are so pleased to see Mattie safe and well. Sissy Seal claps her flippers, as Mattie takes a bow. Mother can't wait to give her little cub a great big furry cuddle.

HOW LONG DO CUBS STAY WITH THEIR MOTHER?

Cubs stay close to their mother at all times until they are about two years old. By then they have learned to hunt, and they may go off on their own.

LATER, BACK IN THEIR DEN, Mother Bear reads her cub a bedtime story. Mattie is so happy in her mother's arms that she falls asleep long before the story's happy ending.

POLAR BEAR

POLAR BEAR CUB

AMERICAN BLACK BEAR

BROWN BEARS

Grizzly bear

Honey bear

Sun bear

Asian black bear

Spectacled bear

33

Here is Mattie with some of her friends. They all live in the
Arctic region, at the top of the world near the North Pole.
Can you see Mattie? Do you recognize all her friends?

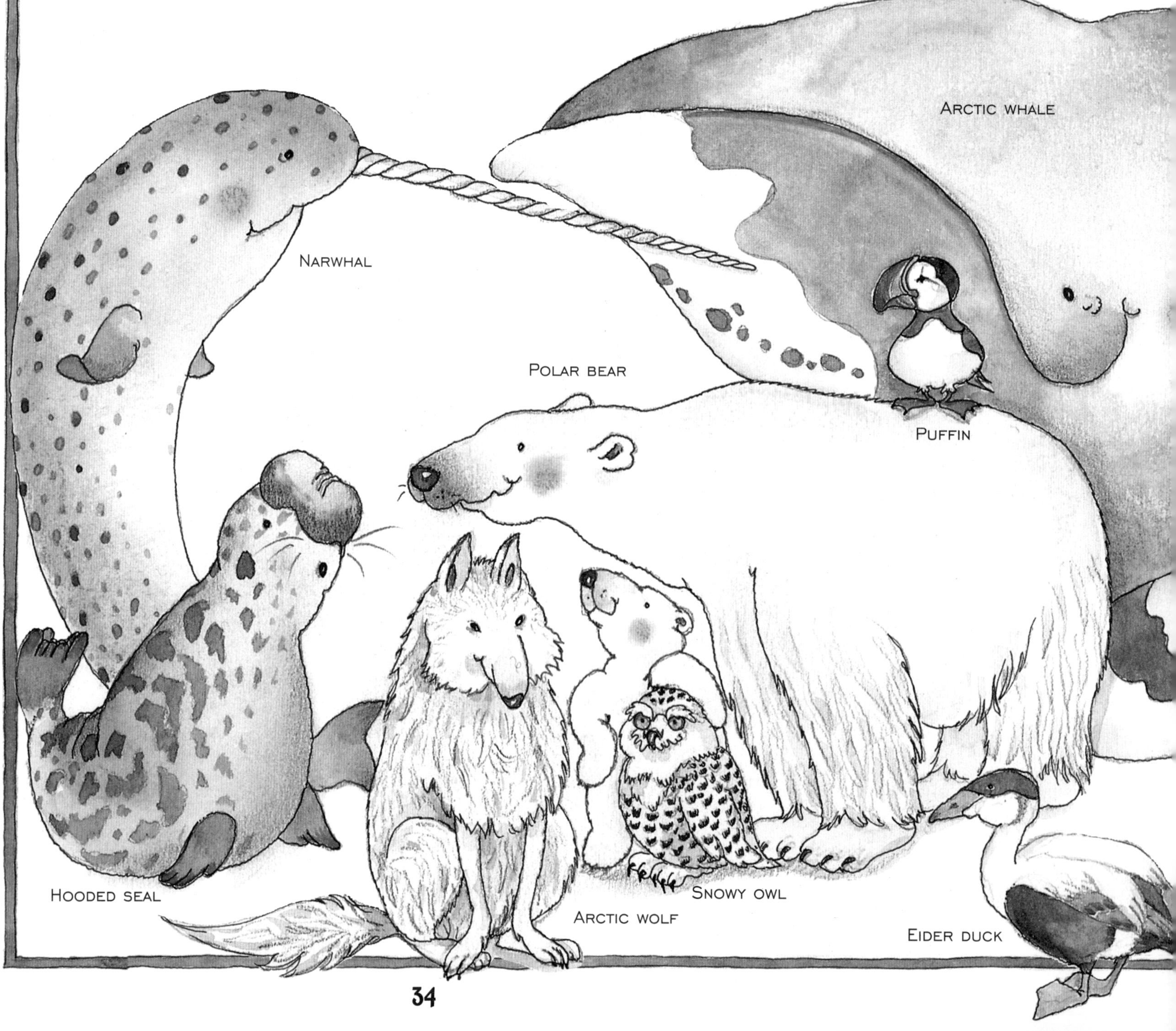

ARCTIC WHALE

NARWHAL

POLAR BEAR

PUFFIN

HOODED SEAL

ARCTIC WOLF

SNOWY OWL

EIDER DUCK

ARCTIC TERN

MATTIE (AND TEDDY)

WALRUS

MUSK OX

RIBBON SEAL

BELUGA (WHITE) WHALE

STOAT

ARCTIC FOX

ARCTIC HARE

LEMMING

35

ARCTIC REGION

GREENLAND

BEAUFORT SEA

LABRADOR SEA

ALASKA

CANADA

UNITED STATES OF AMERICA

PACIFIC OCEAN

ATLANTIC OCEAN

MEXICO

CENTRAL AMERICA

Ben
the Beaver

IN THE BEAVERS' LODGE, Mother Beaver is making a fern-
leaf pie. Her youngest kits are all helping, except for Ben.
He begs his father to take him on the willow expedition.
"Sorry, Ben, you're just too young," Father explains. Ben's older
brothers and sisters chatter eagerly as they get ready to leave.

DO BEAVERS REALLY LIVE IN FAMILIES?

Yes, beavers stay in family groups made up of an adult pair and kits, or young beavers, from several previous years.

WHAT DO BEAVERS EAT?

They eat tender tree bark, tree roots, buds, ferns, grasses, and algae. Beavers are especially fond of poplars and willows.

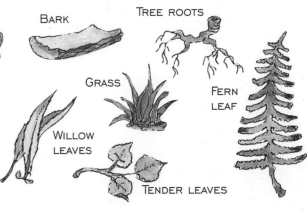

BARK

TREE ROOTS

GRASS

FERN LEAF

WILLOW LEAVES

TENDER LEAVES

It is a beautiful fall evening, as the beavers inside their lodge get ready to set out on their expedition.

DO BEAVERS REALLY LIVE IN LODGES?

Yes, they live in lodges in the middle of ponds.
They even make the pond themselves by building a
dam out of tree trunks and branches. Then they
build their lodge in the middle, where
they are safe from predators.

41

Father Beaver hugs his wife and says goodbye.
"Just raise the red flag if you need anything while
I'm away," he tells her. Then he and the four kits
leave through the underwater door of the lodge.

BEN TRIES TO FOLLOW by sneaking
around the side of the lodge,
but he gets caught up in the sticks.

WHEN BEN UNTANGLES HIMSELF, he sets off after his father and older brothers and sisters. The moon shines down on the lake as Ben swims toward the faint sound of his family's voices. Soon, heavy rain starts to fall.

IN THE WOODS, Father Beaver and the kits are surrounded by eyes peeping out of the leafy darkness. Suddenly, an owl hoots and the kits jump. "Don't worry," Father tells them. "They are all our friends."

BEN REACHES THE SHORE and makes his way through the dark forest. He feels a bit scared until he comes to a well-lit space. Looking around, he's pleased to see that he is surrounded by friends of the forest.

AASHIR, BANU, AND FALAH SQUIRREL

MR. BADGER

GIOVANNI MOUSE

46

KITTY BARN OWL
AND HER CHICKS

SAM AND
CLICKER MOTH

HENRY OTTER

CARLO
RACCOON

MRS. FOX AND DEIRDRE

MR. WOLF

TED CRICKET

BEN

WALLY SKUNK

JANE
POSSUM
WITH BABY
TIM

THE ENTIRE
HARE FAMILY

BANDHURA
PINE MARTEN

CRISPIN BEAR
AND SNOOZER

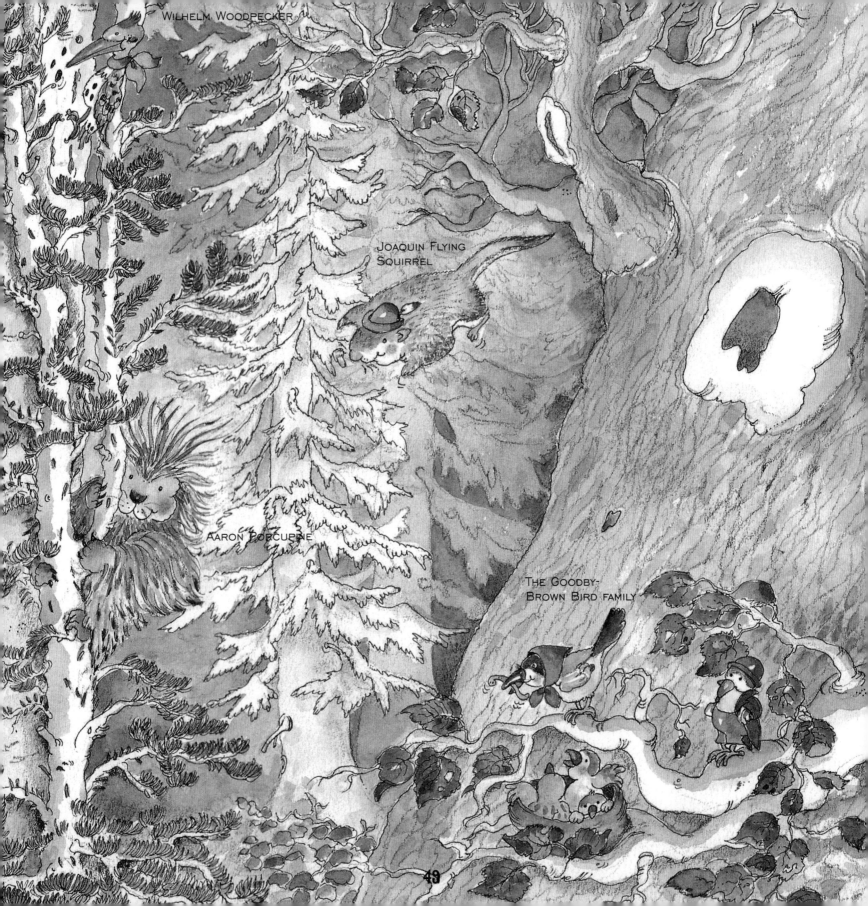

Wilhelm Woodpecker

Joaquin Flying Squirrel

Aaron Porcupine

The Goodby-Brown Bird family

49

DO BEAVERS REALLY FELL TREES?

Yes, they gnaw around the base of the trunk until the tree topples over. Then they use the wood to build dams as well as for food.

DO BEAVERS' TEETH EVER STOP GROWING?

No, their teeth are always growing. So to keep them healthy, beavers have to keep gnawing all the time. This files their teeth down into perfect tools for felling trees and eating.

AFTER SOME TIME Ben catches up with his father and the kits. They are busy collecting willow wood. It starts to rain even harder as Ben climbs a rock and sees their lodge in the distance. "Dad! The red flag!" he yells. "Mom must need help!" Ben feels terrible. If only he had stayed behind with his mother, he could be helping her now. Ben follows close behind as his father and the others race back to the dam.

MOTHER BEAVER AND HER BABIES are
huddled together on top of the
lodge. They clutch their favorite
belongings, but many things have
been swept away. "Don't worry,
little ones," Mother says to
comfort them. "Help
will come soon."

Sure enough, Father Beaver and the kits come floating across the stormy pond on a big log. They are on their way to rescue Mother Beaver and the little ones.

CAN BABY BEAVERS REALLY SWIM?

Yes, kits are able to swim just a few hours after they are born. But they are so small and fluffy at first that it is hard for them to go under water. It takes a while before they can swim down the underwater passage and leave the lodge.

HOW LONG DO KITS STAY IN THE LODGE?

Mother beavers nurse their babies for about six weeks. All members of the family, especially the males, bring food back to the lodge for the kits to eat. Soon the babies start leaving the lodge to swim in the lake, but they come back every morning and sleep through the day. They leave the family lodge when they are about two years old, and it's not long before they start their own families.

53

BEFORE LONG the rain stops and a beautiful rainbow appears. The kits help Father push the big log into the dam, and water stops flooding into the pond. All the beavers give a loud cheer.

HOW BIG IS A BEAVER'S DAM?

A beaver's dam can be anything between 15 and 300 feet (5 and 90 m) long, and it can be up to 10 feet (3 m) tall.

DO BEAVERS REALLY REPAIR THEIR DAMS?

Yes, beavers repair their dams year after year. Some are thought to be hundreds of years old. Most dam-building is done at times of high water in spring and fall.

ALL THE BEAVERS' FRIENDS gather sticks and branches
and carry them across the lake. Some of the beavers'
faraway cousins also come to help. Together they
quickly rebuild the lodge.

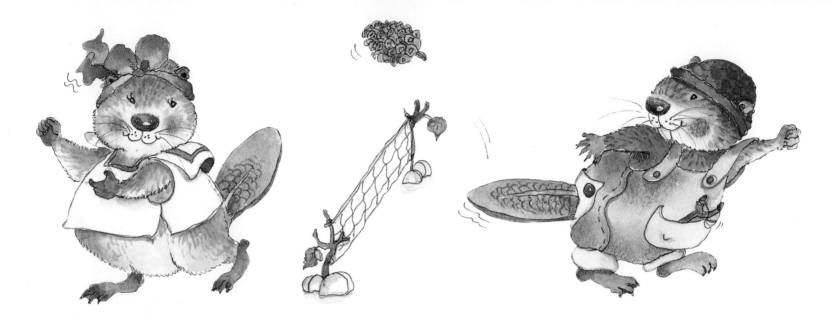

THE BABY BEAVERS are too little to help, but they soon find ways to have fun. Ben and his cousin Natalie play a game of ping-pong with a big lump of weed as a ball. They use their tails as bats!

DO BEAVER FAMILIES WORK TOGETHER TO BUILD THEIR DAMS AND LODGES?

Yes. Adult females are the busiest builders. Kits don't help with construction work until they are at least a year old.

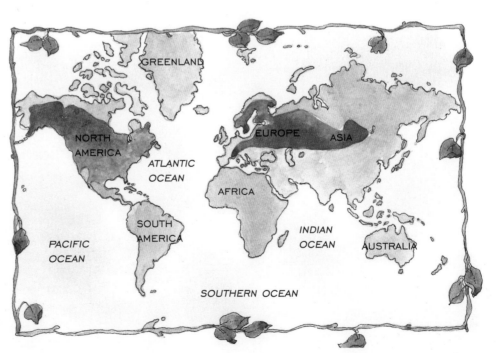

WHERE IN THE WORLD DO BEAVERS LIVE?

As the map shows, beavers live in North America, Scandinavia, western and eastern Europe, central Asia, and northwest China. They were nearly wiped out by hunters in North America, but were reintroduced.

WHEN THE LODGE IS FINISHED, the beavers decide
to have a party. But Ben stays outside and gazes
up at the stars in the night sky. It is nearly winter
and a light dusting of snow covers everything in
sparkling white powder. "Ben, come inside
where it's warm," Father says gently. "The stars
will be there again tomorrow."

INSIDE THE LODGE there is a big party going on, with delicious food to eat and cheerful music to dance to. Everyone is happy to be safely at home again.

Like all beavers, Ben is a rodent. Rodents are a very successful group of animals and there are about 2,000 species of them living in the world today. They live in a wide range of habitats in every part of the world. Many rodents, such as rats and mice, live near humans and are often thought of as pests.

DORMOUSE

SQUIRREL

CHINCHILLA

URSON

NUTRIA

MOUSE

WATER RAT

BEN

GERBIL

HAMSTER

MARMOT

PORCUPINE

Here is Ben with some of his friends. All these animals live in North America. Can you find Ben? Do you recognize all his friends?

CANADA GOOSE

GRIZZLY BEAR

SPRINGHORN

CRANE

ROCKY MOUNTAIN GOAT

SPOONBILL

PRAIRIE DOG

MANATEE

TURTLE

BLACK BEAR

64

GOLDEN EAGLE

BUFFALO

MOOSE

MOUNTAIN LION

COYOTE

RACCOON

BEN

SAGE GROUSE

SKUNK

MOLE

ALLIGATOR

65

Harry

the Wolf

ELK

FRUIT

RABBIT

FOX

WILD SHEEP

FROG

BEAVER

BIRD

MOUSE

CARRION

WHAT DO WOLVES EAT?

Wolves hunt animals such as elk, sheep, rabbits, beavers, mice, and birds. They also eat carrion (dead animals) and wild fruit, including berries.

ONE AFTERNOON, DEEP IN THE FOREST, Mother Wolf and Camilla are picking berries for dinner. Suddenly they hear a strange, whimpering sound coming from the bushes. Mom pulls back some leaves and has a real surprise! There is a little wolf cub, all alone. "Hello," he sobs. "I'm Harry."

WHAT IS THE STORY OF THE WOLF AND ROMULUS AND REMUS?

A famous Roman myth tells of a woman who gave birth to twin sons. Their father was the Roman god, Mars. An enemy of Mars ordered that the two boys be drowned in the River Tiber. Luckily, the servant who was supposed to throw them into the river took pity on the boys and left them on the riverbank. A she-wolf found the boys and adopted them. She took good care of the twins until a shepherd took them into his home. The boys grew up strong and clever. They built a town on the banks of the Tiber where they had been abandoned. This town grew into the great city of Rome.

MOM FEELS VERY SORRY for the little fellow, and she adopts him on the spot. Meanwhile, Uncle Sven has found a skinny chicken that some humans threw out with the trash.

WHAT IS A WOLF PACK?

Wolves live together in groups called packs. The pack is usually made up of a central male and female pair, their cubs (often from several years), and other relatives.

Mom CRADLES HARRY in her arms as she makes her way back to her home in the forest with Camilla and Uncle Sven.

"The rest of our family live just behind that big log,"Mom tells Harry. "We'll be there soon. Then you can rest and eat. You must be very hungry."

THE REST OF THE WOLF PACK is busy preparing dinner. There is lots of work to do. A rabbit is roasting over the fire, and everyone is hoping that Mother Wolf and Uncle Sven will bring back more food.

Mom is sure that all the others will welcome Harry into their family. They are always happy to share their food with others. And the wolf cubs are glad to have lots of friends to play with.

EARLY NEXT MORNING, the wolves are woken
by a terrible rumbling and roaring near their
home. When they go to look, they are horrified at
what they see. The people have come again and
are clearing the forest to make room for their
farms. "What will we do now?" Harry cries.
"Where will we live?"

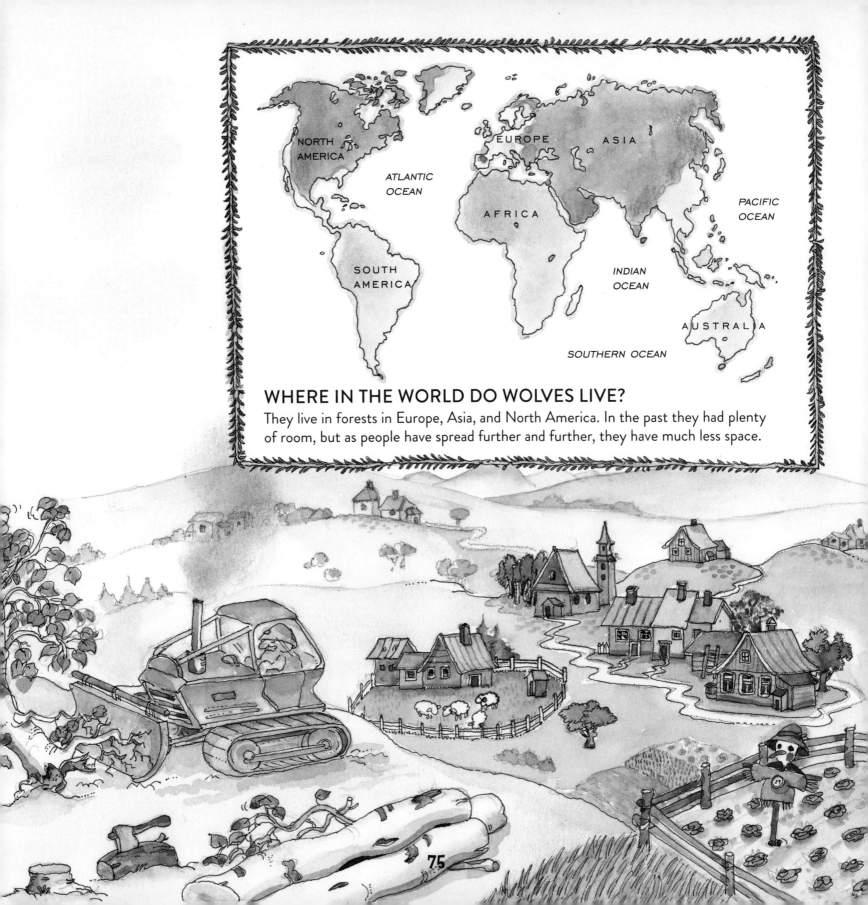

WHERE IN THE WORLD DO WOLVES LIVE?

They live in forests in Europe, Asia, and North America. In the past they had plenty of room, but as people have spread further and further, they have much less space.

NORTH
AMERICA

ATLANTIC
OCEAN

EUROPE

ASIA

AFRICA

PACIFIC
OCEAN

INDIAN
OCEAN

SOUTH
AMERICA

AUSTRALIA

SOUTHERN OCEAN

"WHAT SHOULD WE DO, Mrs. Beaver?" Harry asks.

But Mrs. Beaver doesn't know.

Even Rodney the Mole is stumped.

"What should we do, Mr. Fox?" Harry asks. But Mr. Fox doesn't know either.

Finally, Harry asks George Boar, who tells him to go down to the marshes and speak to Simon the Heron. "He's a great traveler," says George.

76

HOW DO WE KNOW HOW A WOLF FEELS?

Wolves express their feelings using their bodies.

Normal

Alert

Threatening

Dominant

Submissive

Relaxed or completely submissive

"AH WELL," SAYS SIMON, shaking his head. "It's a funny old world, young lad. And it's not getting any bigger!"

But then Simon has an idea. "You could all come north with me," he says. "I'm just leaving, so gather up your things, and we'll be off."

IT IS EVENING by the time the wolves have gathered up all their
belongings and piled them onto a cart. Simon the Heron flies
overhead to show them the way, and the whole pack sets off on the
long journey north. There they hope to find a new, peaceful home.

HARRY IS VERY EXCITED as he marches along
behind Dad, the leader of the pack.

As THE WOLVES travel slowly north, it gets colder and starts to snow. They gradually leave the villages and farmhouses behind. They meet very few other animals, but Sammy Squirrel notices the wolf pack passing by. He waves to them until they are out of sight.

SAMMY
SQUIRREL

ARE THERE DIFFERENT KINDS OF WOLVES?

There is only one species of wolf, but there are many sub-species. They can vary greatly in size and in the color of their pelts. Harry and his friends are gray wolves.

CAN WOLVES REALLY TRAVEL SO FAR?

Wolves can walk and run very well, and they have a lot of stamina. Scientists tracked a wolf pack in Alaska which traveled 700 miles (1,130 km) over a period of six weeks.

RASTA CROW CAWS AT THE PACK as it passes by.
The wolves don't know it, but Rasta is watching
over a mother bear and her newborn cub.
They are safe and warm in their den beneath
the winter snow.

RASTA CROW

83

ALL THE WALKING makes Harry very hungry.
He tries to catch a hedgehog, but soon finds out
how prickly they are! Dad is more successful.
He manages to catch a deer by surprise.

DO WOLF PACKS REALLY HAVE LEADERS?

Yes. Usually the pack has a male and female pair, known as "alpha wolves," who lead. All the other wolves obey them.

HOW DO WOLVES HUNT?

Wolves often hunt alone, but when they want to bring down a large animal, such as a deer, they work together as a team. First they surround their prey, then they close in, leaving no way for their victim to escape.

SIMON THE HERON guides
the wolves to a forest
where they can make
their home. Dad and
Harry lead the way into
a clearing, but just then
a big male wolf appears
among the trees.

WHY DO WOLVES HOWL AT THE MOON?

They howl to claim a piece of land as their territory. It tells other wolves to keep out.

WHAT CAN WE TELL ABOUT A WOLF FROM ITS FACE?

An angry wolf bares its teeth and snarls (left). When it gives way to another wolf, it lowers its ears and closes its mouth (right).

"WHAT ARE YOU DOING HERE?" the big wolf growls. "This is my forest! Get out at once!"

DOES EACH WOLF PACK HAVE ITS OWN TERRITORY?

Generally, yes. Each pack has a territory, and this is the area where the members of the pack hunt for food. The boundaries of the territory may change in different seasons of the year. Outsiders are not welcome and may cause a fight. Sometimes there are lone wolves, who have tried and failed to start a pack of their own.

BUT DAD IS ALSO a big
strong wolf. The two
males start to struggle
and fight.

HARRY JUMPS ABOUT beside them, waving his arms and yelling at the big bad wolf. He helps Dad to win.

89

WHAT HAPPENS WHEN WOLVES FIGHT?

Wolves act a lot like dogs when they meet. First they look at each other.

Then they usually touch noses and sniff each other.

If they don't like what they smell, they begin to snarl.

Then they jump up and start to fight.

When one wolf wins, the other rolls over on its back and submits to the winner.

AT LAST THE WOLVES have a safe new home. Mom and
Aunt Flossie set up camp while Dad and Sven hunt
for food. After a good meal, Mom tucks the cubs
into bed. Harry is very happy but so tired that
he falls fast asleep in Mom's arms.

When the cubs are asleep, Mom and Dad look out over the valley. There is not a farmhouse in sight. "What a great place to raise the cubs," says Mother Wolf.

WHEN ARE WOLF CUBS BORN?

Cubs are usually born in late winter or early spring. At first they stay in a den and feed only on their mother's milk. After a few weeks they start to leave the den. They always go out with their mother or with another adult member of the pack to take care of them. Wolf cubs spend a lot of time sleeping and playing.

Uncle Sven is happy too, while Uncle Jack starts to howl—just to let all the other wolves know that this is their new home.

COYOTE

JACKAL

DID YOU KNOW?

Like all wolves, Harry belongs to the dog family. As well as wolves, wild dogs include foxes, dingos, jackals, and coyotes, and they have spread to every part of the world. They are all quite similar in build, with strong legs and long, bushy tails. Domestic dogs are also part of this family, and scientists believe that they are originally descended from wolves.

RED FOX

FENNEC FOX

ARCTIC FOX

DINGO

MANED WOLF

RACCOON DOG

HARRY

AFRICAN WILD DOG
AND PUPS

93

Here is Harry with many of his friends.
All these animals live in Europe. Can you see
Harry? Do you recognize all his friends?

RED SQUIRREL

CHAMOIS

REINDEER

FALLOW
DEER

GREY
SQUIRREL

WILD BOAR

RABBIT

RED FOX

HEDGEHOG

DESMAN

WOOD MOUSE

HARRY

94

BLUE TITS

BARN OWL

EAGLE OWL

LITTLE OWL

TAWNY OWL

TREE MOUSE

RED DEER

BEAR

IBEX

OTTER

MARMOT

PINE MARTEN

LYNX

POLECAT

PORCUPINE

BADGER

95

EUROPE

ASIA

JAPAN

AFRICA

INDIA

CHINA

PACIFIC OCEAN

INDIAN OCEAN

ATLANTIC
OCEAN

AUSTRALIA

Celia
the Tiger

As soon as Celia is born, deep in the jungle in the heart of India, her mother realizes that she is a little different. Young Celia likes sucking her tail and hugging her teddy cat. In fact, she acts more like a scared little kitten than the daughter of a fearless jungle queen.

HOW DOES A MOTHER TIGER LOOK AFTER HER CUBS?

A mother tiger's two or three cubs are born blind. She carries them gently in her mouth. They start going for short walks with her when they are about four months old. By their first birthday they can hunt for themselves. And when they are two years old they are ready to leave their mother to go off on their own.

99

HOW DOES A TIGER HUNT?

First, the tiger sees its prey, that is, the animal it wants to hunt.

Then the tiger hides in the tall grass ...

MOTHER TIGER DECIDES NOT TO WORRY
that Celia is such a scaredy-cat.
She'll soon learn, Mother thinks, when
I show her how to hunt. "First you must
look for your prey," she tells Celia firmly.

... and suddenly pounces!

The tiger kills its victim with its sharp claws and teeth.

CELIA SPOTS SOME PREY in the nearby bush. But it gives her an awful fright. "Whatever can it be?" wonders Mother, as Celia jumps into her arms.

Oh no! It's just a friendly little mouse causing all the fuss. "Let's leave the hunting for now," sighs Mother.

HOW BIG ARE TIGERS?

Siberian tigers are the biggest. Adult males grow up to nearly 11 feet (3.3 m) long. Females are a bit smaller.

DO TIGERS LIKE TO KEEP CLEAN?

Yes. Tigers spend up to 20 hours a day resting, and for part of this time they lick their fur to keep it clean.

Next, Mother decides to give Celia a swimming lesson. But this doesn't go well either. Unlike all her tiger cousins, Celia is afraid of the water!

DO TIGERS REALLY LIKE WATER?

Yes, unlike many other cats, they do! When it gets very hot, they like to lie in a stream or pool to cool down. They are good swimmers, too.

MOTHER TIGER BEGINS to realize that
she needs help if she is ever to make
Celia fearless. So she invites all her friends
round for a cup of tea and a chat. When
the jungle animals hear about the problem,
they look doubtful and shake their heads.
"You'd better ask the Old Wise One for
advice," they suggest.

Brian Sloth Bear

Mrs Priya
Asian Elephant

Daksh
Cobra

Aaron Tree Shrew

John Hog Badger

107

MR CHITAL SPOTTED DEER, WITH BRITA AND SHIBHI

PRAJEET BLACK PANTHER

MOTHER TIGER

ABIGAIL INDIAN RHINOCEROS

BHARAT CRANE

CELIA

JEEVAN MONGOOSE

BALRAM AND MADHU MACAQUE

WHAT DO TIGERS EAT?

Mostly they eat large animals, such as wild buffalo, pigs, antelope, and deer. But sometimes they catch smaller prey, too, such as monkeys, civets, and prickly porcupines. When they need a snack, they might even catch fish, frogs, crabs, lizards, or snakes.

DEER

WARTHOG

WILD
BUFFALO

FROG

CIVET

MOTHER TIGER AND CELIA climb to the top of a high rock. From there they can see the place where the Old Wise One lives.

ARE SOME TIGERS WHITE?

Very, very occasionally an orange mother tiger has a white cub. White tigers have blue eyes, pink noses, and brown stripes. Some even have no stripes at all. In India, only about twelve white tigers have been seen in the last 100 years.

110

HOW MANY KINDS OF TIGER ARE THERE?

There are only six subspecies, or kinds, of tiger still alive in the wild: the Bengal, Indochinese, Siberian, South China, Malayan, and Sumatran. Even these tigers are endangered and many groups work hard to protect them.

WHERE IN THE WORLD DO TIGERS LIVE?

Tigers live in parts of India, China, Indonesia, and Russia. Some live in hot tropical rainforests, others in cold mountain forests, and some in steamy mangrove swamps.

RUSSIA

CHINA

INDIA

INDONESIA

IT IS NEARLY SUNSET by the time they reach the monkey temple. The Old Wise One listens to Mother Tiger and then gives her advice. "All will be well when the girl finds a friend," she says wisely.

NEXT MORNING, Mother Tiger goes off early to hunt for breakfast. When Celia wakes up to find she is all alone, she jumps out of bed and rushes off to search for her mother.

But Celia has a nasty shock when
she falls straight into a hole!

115

It's NOT just any old
hole. It's a trap left
by human hunters.

Now Celia is well and truly stuck!
Luckily, Rhino the baby rhinoceros
sees what happened. But can he help?

RHINO FETCHES A ROPE and uses all
his strength to pull Celia out.

Together they wait for
Mother Tiger to come back
with breakfast.

118

LATER THAT DAY, Mother says Celia can go and
play with Rhino. They are both happy and have
fun in the jungle.

HOW DO TIGERS KEEP THEIR CLAWS SHARP?

They scratch them on tree trunks. When
they walk, they pull their claws into their
toes so they don't wear down.

IN FACT, CELIA IS SO BUSY having fun
that she soon learns how to hunt and swim.
With Rhino around, she's not scared any more.

WHY DO TIGERS HAVE STRIPES?
So they can hide in tall grass when they are hunting. The stripes help
to break up their outline. No two tigers have the same pattern of stripes!

Mother Tiger watches happily
as Celia and Rhino play together.
The Old Wise One was right about friends.
And now Celia plays some very daring games!

WILD CAT

GEOFFROY'S CAT

GOLDEN CAT

PUMA

LYNX

LION

DID YOU KNOW?

All cats, both big and small, belong to one family. Most cats—except lions—like to hunt on their own at night. The main difference between big cats like tigers and lions, and small cats, such as our domestic cats, is that the little ones can purr, while the big ones can roar.

OCELOT

CHEETAH

LEOPARD

CELIA

PALM CIVET

FLYING SQUIRREL

Here is Celia with her many new friends. They all live in Asia. How many do you recognize?

GAUR

CHITAL (AXIS DEER)

SUN BEAR

INDIAN RHINOCEROS

TARSIER

TAPIR

GIANT PANDA

ORANGUTAN

HIMALAYAN TAHR

LIZARD

SHREW

124

GIBBON

PEACOCK

BAT

BACTRIAN CAMEL

ASIAN ELEPHANT

PYTHON

SARUS CRANE

PANTHER

MONGOOSE

CELIA

HAMSTER

MONITOR LIZARD

ATLANTIC OCEAN

COLOMBIA

VENEZUELA

GUYANA

SURINAME

FRENCH GUIANA

BRAZIL

ECUADOR

PERU

BOLIVIA

PACIFIC OCEAN

CHILE

URUGUAY

ARGENTINA

Josh
the Anteater

IT IS A BRIGHT, sunny morning on the South American
grasslands, and Josh and his mother are having breakfast.

WHAT DO ANTEATERS EAT?

Ants, of course! And termites. The ants and termites live in tall mounds that dot the grasslands. An anteater can eat up to 30,000 of these insects and their eggs in one day!

HOW LONG IS AN ANTEATER'S TONGUE?

It's up to 24 inches (60 cm) long! The anteater flicks it in and out of holes in the mound, and the ants stick to it.

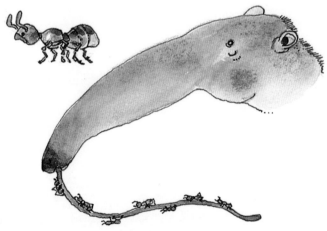

TODAY IS A VERY SPECIAL DAY for Josh. His mother has promised to take him to the big market that is held far away in the Andes mountains.

IT'S A LONG AND DANGEROUS JOURNEY from the grasslands up into the mountains. After a steep climb, Josh and his mother can see the market on the other side of a deep valley. They have to cross a wobbly rope bridge to get there.

HOW DOES AN ANTEATER CARRY HER CUB?

A mother anteater lets her cub ride piggyback. If the cub falls off, it makes a shrill grunt to let its mother know!

THEY MAKE IT SAFELY ACROSS and find
themselves in a noisy, colorful crowd.
The air is full of the smell of freshly
baked honey-and-ant fritters and the
sweet sound of flute music. Josh asks his
mother if she will buy him a flute.

131

THE NEXT DAY AT SCHOOL, Josh takes out his new flute and shows it to his friends. They all crowd around to listen as he gently blows into it through his nose. The only one missing is Josh's best friend Dillo the armadillo, who is off sick.

PANGOLIN

WHO ARE THESE STRANGE CREATURES?

Like anteaters, the scaly pangolin and the donkey-eared, pig-nosed aardvark both eat ants and termites. But they live far away from anteaters. Pangolins live in Africa and Asia, and aardvarks live in Africa.

AARDVARK

AFTER SCHOOL, Josh rushes off to visit his friend Dillo. The armadillos live on the pampas, or dry plains, just beyond the rainforest.

WHY DO ANTEATERS SNIFF SO MUCH?

Anteaters can't see very well, so they find things with their noses. They sniff the ground to find their way about.

Josh says hello to Mother Armadillo and shows her his flute. Then he gives her a basket of goodies that his mother made for Dillo's large family.

DILLO IS IN BED, and he's not feeling very well at all. Josh plays him a tune on his flute, but he isn't very good yet and sometimes blows notes out of tune. Dillo starts to giggle. Josh's music makes him feel much better.

WHAT IS A RAINFOREST?

It is a warm, wet forest where giant trees tower above smaller trees, and it almost never stops raining! Millions of animals live there, from shrieking birds and monkeys to huge snakes and creepy-crawly insects.

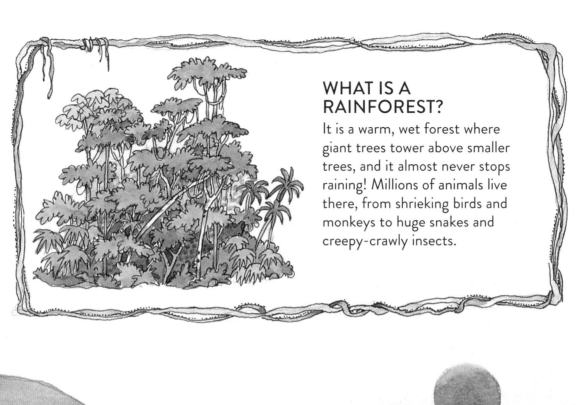

LATER, JOSH WAVES GOODBYE to the
armadillos and heads off home
through the rainforest.

WHY DO ANTEATERS WALK IN SUCH A CLUMSY WAY?

Anteaters can't put their front feet flat because their curved claws are too long. Instead, they walk on their outer knuckles, and this makes them lumber along.

ENRICO BOA
CONSTRICTOR

FEDERICO AND WALTER
WOOLLY MONKEY

ANGELO AND
TINA PECCARY

ANTONIA
AND SARA
CAPYBARA

JOSH FEELS WORRIED in the noisy rainforest. He sees lots of different animals in the trees and on the forest floor. He tries not to trip over the big tree roots and not to walk into the vines hanging down from the branches.

JOE THREE-TOED SLOTH

TERRY TREE PORCUPINE

TILLY AND TOT
TOUCAN

STEFANO
SILKY ANTEATER

HUMMER
AND BUZZ
HUMMINGBIRD

JILLY JAGUAR

ARNOLDO
AND
ARTURO
AGOUTI

142

Orazio Two-Toed Sloth

Filippo Macaw

Pedro Parrot

Barry Bat

Timo Tamandua

Juan Turtle

143

SUDDENLY A GIANT
ANACONDA slides out of
the swampy water
and gives Josh a
shock. He runs off
as fast as he can.

CAN ANTEATERS GO FAST?
Anteaters usually shuffle along
slowly, but they can move quickly
if they are frightened.

THEN AN EAGLE swoops down
with her sharp talons out.
Josh only just escapes.

CAN ANTEATERS SWIM?
Yes, they are very good swimmers.
They often take a dip in South
America's mighty Amazon River.

IN HIS PANIC, Josh runs straight toward a fierce, roaring jaguar. It gives him such a fright that he falls over. Who can save him now?

THAT'S LUCKY! Looking up, Josh is amazed to see his mother waving her sharp claws at the big cat. Mother came to look for him, and he has never seen her look so fierce! She is certainly too scary for the jaguar.

WHAT DO ANTEATERS USE THEIR CLAWS FOR?

If threatened, an anteater will stand up and use its long, sharp claws to defend itself. It also uses them to tear open termite mounds and anthills.

DO ANTEATERS SLEEP MUCH?

Yes. Giant anteaters sleep at night, but they don't sleep deeply. Even a small noise will wake them. So they also like to have lots of naps during the day. They curl up under their long, bushy tails to keep warm.

ON THE WAY HOME, Josh is so tired that Mother Anteater has to carry him. He falls fast asleep and is soon dreaming of crispy fried ants, fresh from his mother's oven.

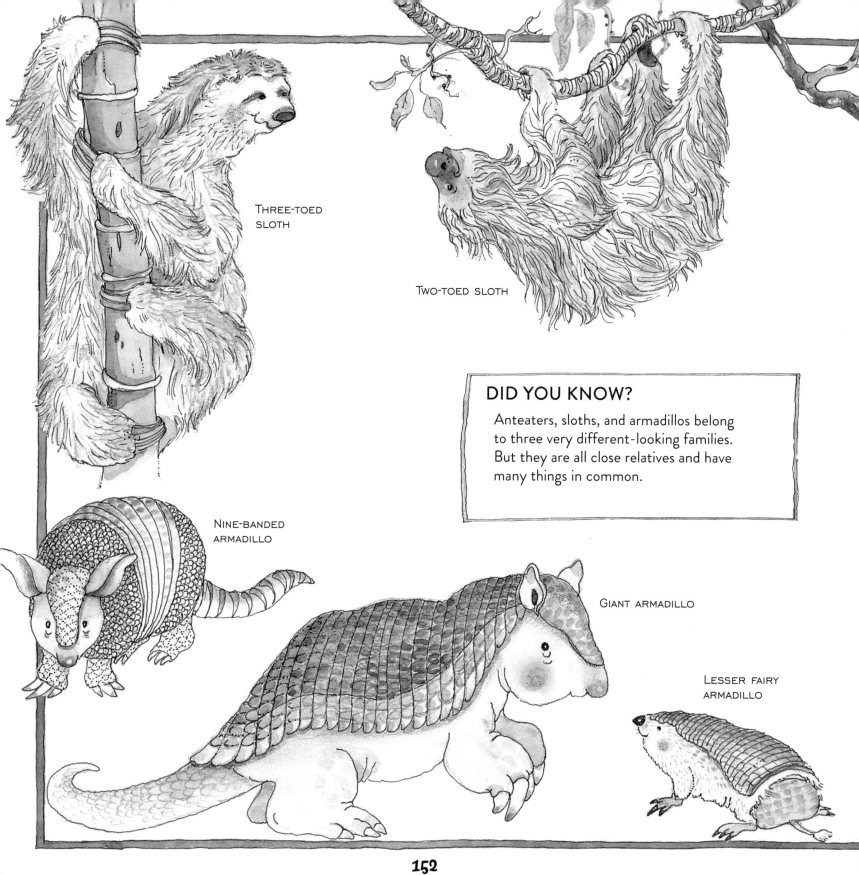

THREE-TOED SLOTH

TWO-TOED SLOTH

DID YOU KNOW?

Anteaters, sloths, and armadillos belong to three very different-looking families. But they are all close relatives and have many things in common.

NINE-BANDED ARMADILLO

GIANT ARMADILLO

LESSER FAIRY ARMADILLO

SILKY ANTEATER

TAMANDUA

JOSH

HAIRY ARMADILLO

153

TOUCAN

THREE-TOED SLOTH

BOA CONSTRICTOR

SPECTACLED BEAR

Here is Josh with many of the animals he knows.
They all live in Central or South America.
How many of his friends do you recognize?

BAT

CONDOR

PATAGONIAN
HARE

TAPIR

CAPYBARA

PECCARY

154

HUMMINGBIRD

TREE PORCUPINE

TAMANDUA

VICUÑA

LLAMA

SPIDER
MONKEY

BLUE
AND
YELLOW
MACAW

CHINCHILLA

JOSH

JAGUAR

RHEA

LESSER FAIRY
ARMADILLO

GIANT ARMADILLO

ANACONDA

POISON DART
FROG

TORTOISE

155

SPAIN

MEDITERRANEAN SEA

RED SEA

AFRICA

ATLANTIC OCEAN

INDIAN OCEAN

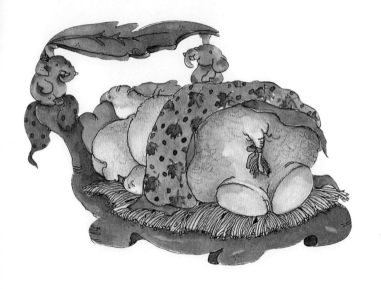

Lizzie
the Elephant

IN A SHADY ACACIA GROVE on the African
savanna, Grandma Elephant is serving tea.
Mom says she has some very good news. She is
expecting a new baby! Mom's daughter Chloe just
goes on sucking her trunk happily.

DO BABY ELEPHANTS REALLY SUCK THEIR TRUNK?

Yes, just as human babies sometimes suck their thumb for comfort, elephant babies—called calves—may suck their trunk.

DO FEMALE ELEPHANTS REALLY LIVE TOGETHER IN A GROUP?

Yes, they live together in a family herd led by an older female, called a matriarch. Female elephants, or cows, help each other to protect and bring up their young.

ONE RAINY DAY quite soon after, Mom is ready to give birth. Grandma stands over her with an umbrella.

Aunt Flo, Aunt Flora, and the girls all gather around ready to help.

161

AT LAST THE BABY ELEPHANT IS BORN. It's a girl!
Grandma is pleased and Mom feels tired and
happy as she cuddles her new daughter, Lizzie.
Chloe is thrilled to have a new sister.

WHEN ARE ELEPHANT CALVES BORN?
In the rainy season, when there is lots of
new grass for the mother elephant to eat.

A FEW DAYS LATER, Grandma and Mom take Lizzie and Chloe out into the bush. They show the youngsters the tastiest plants to eat, and Lizzie quickly learns how to use her trunk. Grandma also warns them about poisonous plants and dangerous animals.

WHAT DO ELEPHANTS EAT?

They eat grass, leaves, shrubs, twigs, flowers, fruit, and bark. They use their trunks to gather food and carry it to their mouths.

DO ELEPHANTS REALLY WASH THEMSELVES?

Yes, elephants have sensitive skins and the cool water is soothing. They like to roll in mud, then suck up water in their trunks and spray it over themselves and their friends!

DO THEY TAKE DUST BATHS TOO?

Yes, the dust also makes their skin feel good, and it helps to keep ticks and fleas away.

MOM

GRANDMA

CHLOE

EVERY DAY LIZZIE and her family go to the waterhole to drink and bathe. Lizzie runs on ahead and jumps straight into the water. Aunt Flora always brings her beauty case, and a scrubbing brush to clean the girls.

166

AUNT FLO, TAKING A DUST BATH

AUNT FLORA

ZOE

LIZZIE

167

SEBASTIAN LEOPARD

TERRY ANTELOPE

JED AND MYRA BABOON

VINCENT AND RACHEL WARTHOG

THE ELEPHANTS ARE NOT the only ones at the watering hole. All the animals gather at dawn and dusk to drink and gossip.

FLIP AND FLAP EGRET

FRED MARABOU

FLORA
GIRAFFE

WINSTON
GIRAFFE

FANNY AND
DAVE RHINO

169

After her bath Lizzie wanders off to gather flowers. She hums as she goes, and chases pretty butterflies far into the bush.

WHY DO BIRDS FOLLOW ELEPHANTS AS THEY WALK THROUGH THE BUSH?

Because the elephants disturb insects and other small animals, which the birds feed on.

BACK AT HOME, everyone is worried about Lizzie. Where can she be? Mom makes long, low-pitched noises to call for her daughter.

WHAT IS AN ELEPHANT ROAD?

It is a wide path through the bush made by elephants. They use the same path for generations, so it becomes deep and well-marked.

DO ELEPHANTS REALLY CALL EACH OTHER?

Yes, elephants can communicate with each other over quite long distances. They use rumbling calls that are so low-pitched that people cannot hear them.

171

WHY DO BIRDS SIT ON ELEPHANTS' BACKS?

Birds such as cattle egrets and oxpeckers ride along on elephants so that they can peck insects and ticks from their thick skin.

LITTLE LIZZIE is too far away to hear her mother calling. She sits in the shade of a large rock to rest for a while. She enjoys sticking pretty petals on her toenails and chattering with the birds. Lizzie is too busy to notice time passing by.

SOON IT IS EVENING and Lizzie suddenly sees an enormous elephant approaching. He is so big and heavy that the ground shakes as he walks. Lizzie feels scared, but the elephant roars, "Hello, you must be Lizzie! I'm your grandpa, and a little bird told me that your mother is searching everywhere for you."

173

LIZZIE IS HAPPY to meet her grandfather, and she skips along beside him as they make their way home together. But suddenly Grandpa Elephant stops and points his walking stick at some bones beside the path. "Look, Lizzie," he says gently. "Those bones belong to your great-grandmother. She was a brilliant leader and a very wise elephant indeed. You must try to be more like her, and never go running off on your own."

DO ELEPHANTS REALLY RECOGNIZE BONES?

Apparently, yes! They will often stop when they see elephant bones, touching them with their trunks and sometimes tossing them into the air.

When Grandpa and Lizzie at last get back to the rest of family, they see Mom, Aunt Flo, and Aunt Flora huddling around Chloe and Zoe.

Grandma is bravely waving her umbrella at a lion hiding in a nearby bush. "Shoo! Leave us alone!" shouts Grandma.

GRANDPA ELEPHANT QUICKLY joins in. He rushes
toward the lion, bellowing and shaking his stick.
This scares the lion and he soon runs away.

WHAT DO DUNG BEETLES DO?

Seeds that an elephant eats pass through it and come out in its dung. The beetles carry the seeds underground in little balls of dung, and the seeds then grow into plants.

DO ELEPHANTS REALLY RUB THEIR TRUNKS TOGETHER?

Yes. When elephants meet, they stand close together and entwine their trunks. They also give each other comforting pats with their trunks throughout the day.

EVERYONE IS PLEASED to see Lizzie safe and sound. They decide at once to have a family party. Grandma and Grandpa haven't seen each other for ages and wrap their trunks together in greeting.

DID YOU KNOW?

There are two species, or different kinds, of elephant. One lives in Africa and is called the African elephant (above). The other species lives in India and Southeast Asia and is known as the Asian elephant (next page). African elephants are bigger than their Asian cousins, have larger ears, and both males and females have tusks.

DID YOU KNOW?

Among Asian elephants, usually only the males have tusks. In Asia, some elephants are used for work, such as hauling logs, or for transport. In India, elephants are often dressed in brightly colored materials and take part in religious parades and festivals.

CHIMPANZEE

GIRAFFE

PANGOLIN

OSTRICH

ANTELOPE

ZEBRA

BUSH BABY

FLAMINGO

LIZZIE

MARABOU

HYENA

DESERT
HEDGEHOG

BABOON

CROCODILE

184

Here is Lizzie with some of her friends. All these animals live in Africa. Can you find Lizzie? Do you recognize all her friends?

LEOPARD

CAMEL

AFRICAN BUFFALO

VULTURE

RHINOCEROS

GORILLA

HIPPOPOTAMUS

GERBIL

LION

GUINEA FOWL

CHAMELEON

BUSHPIG

Buster
the Kangaroo

EARLY ONE MORNING, deep in the Australian
outback, Buster gets ready to jump into his
mother's safe, warm pouch. He does this every
day, but this time Mother Kangaroo won't let
him. "No, Buster, you're a big boy now!" she
says. "And soon you'll have a new baby sister.
She is growing in my pouch right now."

DO BABY KANGAROOS REALLY GROW IN THEIR MOTHERS' POUCHES?

Yes. When kangaroos are born, they are very small and helpless. The tiny creatures clamber into their mother's pouch, where they are safe and warm. They drink milk to help them grow.

HOW LONG DO THEY STAY IN THE POUCH?

For several months. And even after they leave the pouch, they still feed by drinking their mother's milk.

BUSTER IS VERY CROSS with his mother, and he's annoyed with his new baby sister, even though he hasn't seen her yet. He remembers when he used to bound across the desert, tucked safely inside his mother's pouch.

WHAT IS A MOB?

A mob is a large group of kangaroos—sometimes up to 50 or more—that live together. Not all kangaroos live in mobs, but most of the larger kinds do.

It was always such fun in the pouch. Buster used to smile and wave at all his young friends in the mob.

BUSTER WAS USED to doing everything with his mother.
When the rains come, the dry desert is filled with
tender green grass and pretty flowers.

MOTHER KANGAROO showed Buster which were the best types of shoots and leaves to eat. That's how he learned which ones were tastiest.

WHAT DO KANGAROOS EAT?
Most kangaroos eat grass, leaves, roots, seeds, and fruit. A few of the smaller species also feed on insects.

HOW DO KANGAROOS MOVE?

Kangaroos have large, powerful hind legs that power them along as they hop through the bush and desert. At full speed, they can travel at more than 35 mph (56 km/h).

Now Buster is sad that he has to do things all on his own. Rob and Tina Wombat try to comfort him, but even they can't cheer him up.

THEN BUSTER HAS AN IDEA. "I know, I'll run away," he says to Rob and Tina. Before they can stop him, he puts a few things in his backpack and hops off through the bush as fast as he can.

BUSTER HOPS ON AND ON, through the bush, over the
grasslands, and across the burning red desert sands.
But the outback is huge. It seems never-ending.

APARI EMU

KADEE EMU

BERRINIGAR AND
DAREL EMU

JANNALI EMU

196

BUSTER STARTS TO WONDER where he will end up.
On his way he passes a family of emus. But he
thinks he had better hop on.

THEN BUSTER PASSES some desert animals he has
never seen before. One of the lizards has a big frill
around his neck, and another is spiny all over.

KAMI FRILLED LIZARD

JOHN MARSUPIAL MOUSE

THE LIZARDS AND OTHER ANIMALS would like to ask Buster where he's off to. But before they can stop him, he has hopped out of sight.

MIKE MOLOCH

ERIK AND TAMMY ECHIDNA

HOW DO KANGAROOS KEEP CLEAN?

Kangaroos sometimes go in the water, but usually to keep cool rather than to stay clean. They use the claws on their short front legs to remove pests and groom themselves.

IT IS STARTING TO GET DARK when
Buster reaches a small pool.
He says hello to the cockatoos and other birds,
before joining them in a welcome drink.

200

ARE KANGAROOS AFRAID OF OTHER ANIMALS?

Apart from humans, the only animals kangaroos fear are dingos and eagles. Dingos (like the one above) are a type of wild dog.

BUSTER HAS BEEN HOPPING all day and is very tired. He lies down beside a warm rock, and playful little bats fly around him. Before he falls asleep, Buster decides that tomorrow he will try to find his cousin Gray, who lives far away in the forest.

BUSTER SETS OFF early next morning. He soon meets a friendly group of koalas, who invite him to have breakfast in their gum tree.

But as Buster sits sipping his tea, his nose begins to twitch. What is that strange smell?

203

It's SMOKE! The gum tree is on fire! All the animals start to jump, fly, and scramble down the trees. Anything to avoid the flames and smoke. Buster climbs down as fast as he can and runs for his life.

WHAT HAPPENS TO THE BUSH AFTER A FIRE?

Bush and forest fires are common in Australia, and the local trees and plants can usually survive them. Often the fire passes over them quickly and only burns the leaves. After a few months, the bush recovers.

206

BUSTER AND HIS NEW FRIENDS
soon reach a stream. Buster hops
into the cool water. Just then the wind
changes, blowing the fire in a different
direction. Buster is safe, and he makes
more new friends—Terence and
Teresa **Platypus** and their family.

BUSTER SOON HOPS OFF AGAIN. He travels though the bush until he suddenly hears loud stomping noises up ahead. He peeps around a tree and sees two kangaroos having a boxing match. And one of them is Cousin Gray!

"HI, COUSIN," cries Buster. The two young kangaroos hug each other. "Come on," says Gray. "Let's get back to the mob."

DO KANGAROOS REALLY BOX?

Yes, they do. Male kangaroos fight each other over female mates. They stand upright facing each other, then lock arms and try to push each other backward. We call this "boxing."

Gray puts his arm around Buster and the two set off, chatting and giggling.

HOW DO KANGAROOS TALK TO EACH OTHER?

Kangaroos are not noisy animals. Adult males hiss and spit while fighting. Females make clicking sounds to call their young.

As the two young kangaroos get close to a clearing in the bush, they hear the excited chatter of the mob. But what a surprise for Buster!

210

His mother is there waiting for him, and his
new baby sister is peeping out of her pouch.
Buster is so pleased to see them both, and
Mother Kangaroo is delighted to have him back.

VIRGINIA OPOSSUMS

WOMBAT

BUSTER

DID YOU KNOW?

Like all kangaroos, Buster is a marsupial. Female marsupials are different from all other animals because they have a pouch on their stomach in which they carry their babies. Most marsupials live in Australia and New Zealand. One or two species live in the Americas, mainly in the south. All the animals on these two pages are marsupials.

NUMBAT

TASMANIAN DEVIL

Rat kangaroo

Bandicoot

Koala

Honey possum

Wallaby

Marsupial mole

FLYING POSSUM

BATS

Here is Buster with some of his friends.
They all live in Australia and New Zealand.
Can you find Buster?
Do you recognize all his friends?

KOALA

EASTERN QUOLL

EMU

BUSTER

DINGO

WALLABY

BLACK SWAN

PLATYPUS

WOMBAT

MOLOCH

ECHIDNA

FRILLED LIZARD

PENGUIN

PINK COCKATOO

BIRD OF PARADISE

SUGAR GLIDER

FLYING SQUIRREL

FEATHERTAIL GLIDER

GRAY KANGAROO

CASSOWARY

PARROT

ECHIDNA

QUOLL

KIWI

TUATARA

CROCODILE

MARSUPIAL MOUSE

TASMANIAN DEVIL

215

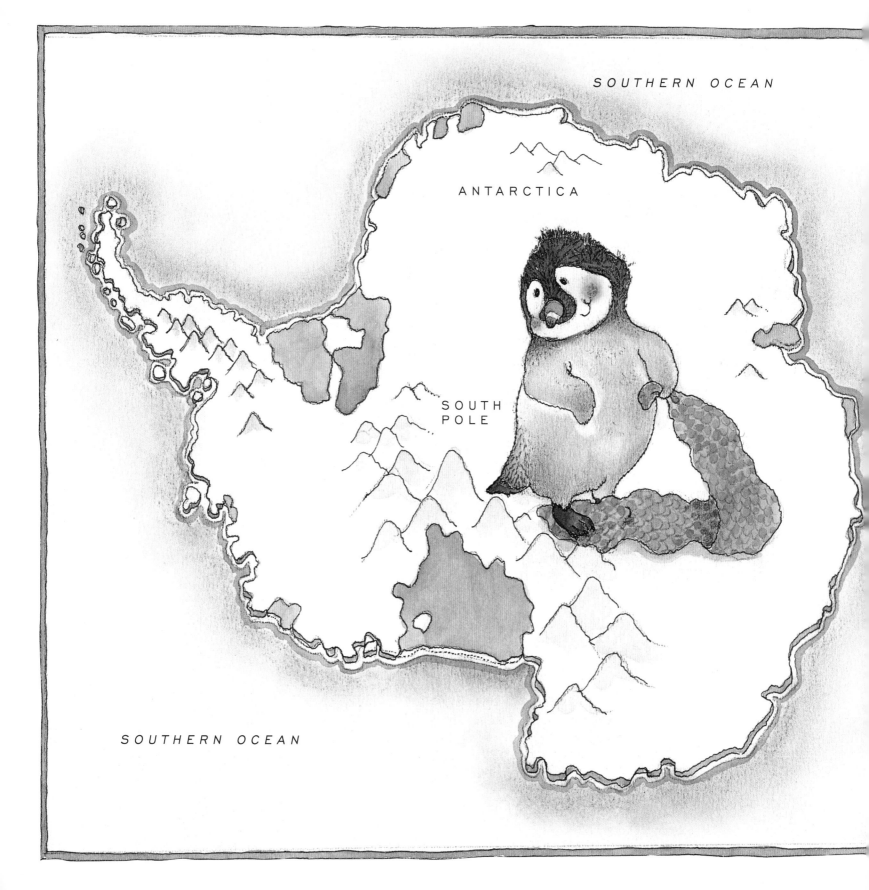

SOUTHERN OCEAN

ANTARCTICA

SOUTH
POLE

SOUTHERN OCEAN

Bob
the Penguin

ARE PENGUINS REALLY BIRDS?

Yes, they certainly are birds. Their body is covered with feathers, but they cannot fly. All the different kinds live near the cold coasts of southern oceans.

Every fall the emperor penguins set off south on the long journey to their meeting place near the South Pole. They march along day after day across the ice and snow. Alfred has been on this march many times, but this year he finds it more tiring than ever. "I'm getting too old for this," he says, but soon he's on the move again.

AT LAST THEY ARRIVE at the meeting place and the penguin party is soon in full swing. It's good to meet up with old friends after such a long journey, and suddenly Alfred spots a very special friend in the crowd.

WHY DO EMPEROR PENGUINS WALK SO FAR?

They may travel more than 60 miles (100 km) across the ice to reach their breeding grounds. Once there, females pick a male penguin to be their mate so that they can start a family together.

FLORA IS WEARING a purple shawl and Alfred thinks she looks even prettier than last year. He is so happy to see her that he spills his drink. Then he whistles happily, hoping that Flora hasn't forgotten their special tune.

221

DO EMPEROR PENGUINS BUILD A NEST?

No, they keep their egg warm in a different way. After she lays the egg, the female passes it to the male, who holds it on his feet under a fold of skin. This space is called a brood pouch. Then the female can go off to feed. When the egg has hatched, the male passes the chick back to his mate.

ALFRED TRIES TO IMPRESS FLORA by bowing politely and nodding his head. At first Flora looks the other way, but then she bows too and the couple waddle off together. Alfred is pleased that his special friend has chosen him. Soon Flora will lay an egg and the proud parents will have an emperor chick!

WHEN THE CHICK HAS HATCHED from the egg, his parents decide to call him Bob. Flora and Alfred take it in turns to look after their chick. They both get very tired and need to walk a long way to the coast to catch some fish and feed. They take that in turns, too, so that they both keep their strength up.

HOW MANY EGGS DOES AN EMPEROR PENGUIN LAY?

A female emperor penguin lays just one egg each year, in May or June. The egg is about 5 inches (13 cm) long.

HOW DO PENGUIN CHICKS KEEP WARM?

Chicks have thick, fluffy down feathers that keep them warm in the early weeks. At about seven weeks they lose their gray down and grow adult feathers.

POOR LITTLE BOB feels very cold. His mother says this is most unfortunate because they live in the coldest part of the world!

BUT FLORA FEELS SORRY for her chick and gives him a blanket. When that isn't enough, she wonders what to do. Then she has a brilliant idea!

Flora decides to knit a warm outfit for little Bob. First she makes him a wonderful onesie. Then she knits him a long, thick scarf. Bob helps his mother so she'll finish the scarf more quickly.

Now Bob is the warmest chick in the whole colony!

HOW DO PENGUINS FEED THEIR CHICKS?

Emperor parents take turns to go off and catch fish and other sea creatures. They eat some themselves and store the rest in their crop, a pouch in the gullet. Later, they can bring this food up into their throat to feed the chick.

227

HOW BIG ARE EMPEROR PENGUINS?

Emperor chicks are small, but they grow into the biggest penguins of all. As adults they reach a height of about 4 feet (1.2 m) and weigh 75 pounds (34 kg) or more.

228

FLORA HAD ANOTHER REASON for knitting Bob's bright green scarf. She thought it would help her find him in the crowded colony. There's lots going on today. But where is Bob?

AH, THERE'S BOB, in the playground. Everyone seems to be having fun, but why is Bob hiding under the slide?

Despite all his parents' efforts, he is a very shy little penguin and he hasn't made any friends yet.

BOB IS HIDING as usual when an icy snow storm blows up. The parents have all gone fishing, so the chicks huddle together to keep warm. But Bob is too late and he's stuck at the edge of the crowd, where it's freezing. It's lucky he is wearing his green scarf.

HOW CAN FEATHERS KEEP PENGUINS WARM?

Penguins have short, hollow feathers. They are bent over so that one lies on top of another, overlapping like roof tiles to make a waterproof covering. Penguins have more feathers than most birds and grow new ones every year.

DO PENGUINS REALLY HUDDLE TOGETHER?

Emperor penguins do. They form a huddle to escape wind chill and conserve warmth. They take turns to stand at the most exposed part on the outside.

233

ONCE THE SNOW STORM is over, Bob feels
a bit warmer. He made some friends in
the huddle, and now he has fun playing
games with them. But Bob's not used to
games. He goes too near the edge of an
ice cliff and suddenly finds himself
heading beak-first for the sea!

**ARE PENGUINS GOOD
SWIMMERS?**

Yes, they are fast, skillful swimmers.
They use their flippers to propel
themselves and their feet as rudders.
Penguins can dive down very deep
and have good underwater vision.

234

BOB MAKES A BIG SPLASH when he hits the water. He has never tried to swim before, so he'll have to learn fast! The other penguins fear the worst when they see a big leopard seal heading straight for Bob. "That chick will make a tasty snack," the seal thinks. Who can save Bob now?

HOW MANY PENGUINS ARE THERE IN A COLONY?

There may be more than 20,000 pairs of birds in an emperor penguin colony. A breeding colony, where males and females find mates, is called a rookery.

Bob is very lucky! The petrel who was resting on the icy cliff is too quick for the leopard seal. The big bird dives down and rescues Bob in the nick of time.

DO ANY BIRDS ATTACK PENGUINS?

The skua (right) will try to snatch emperor penguin chicks, and it has even been known to attack adult penguins. As its name suggests, the South Polar skua flies all the way to the South Pole.

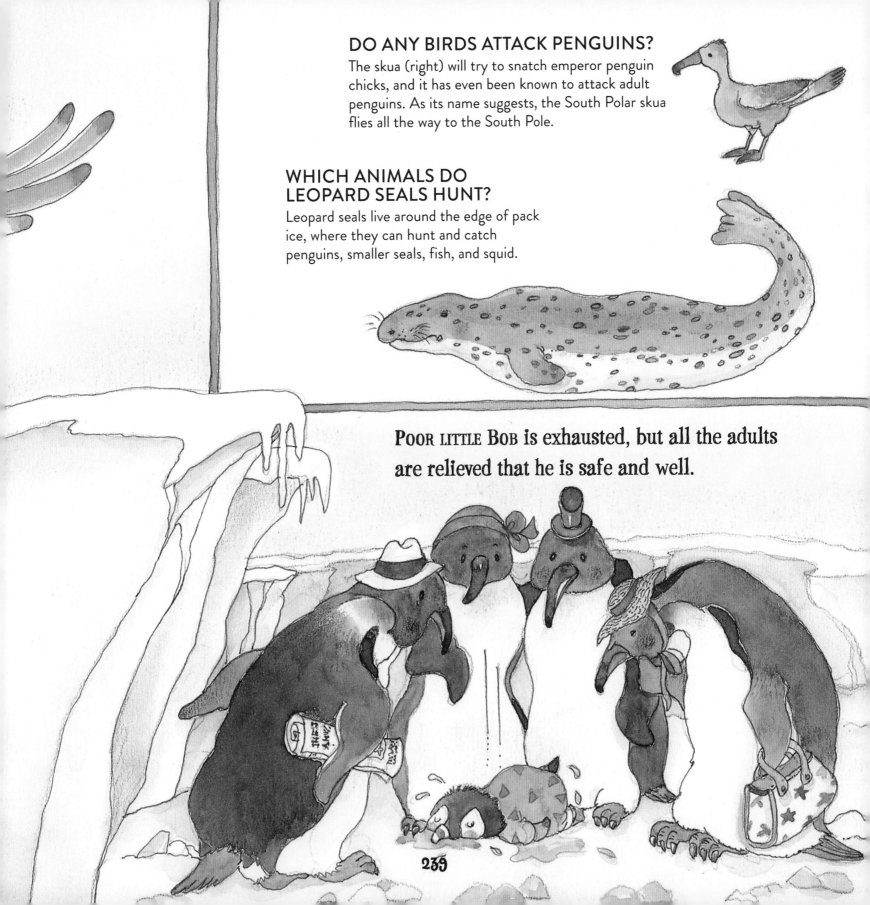

WHICH ANIMALS DO LEOPARD SEALS HUNT?

Leopard seals live around the edge of pack ice, where they can hunt and catch penguins, smaller seals, fish, and squid.

POOR LITTLE BOB is exhausted, but all the adults are relieved that he is safe and well.

Now THAT IT'S SUMMER again, the penguins, seals, gulls, and other animals enjoy the sunshine at the Antarctic coast. Bob is warm at last, and his mother is relaxed and happy. In a few months it will be time for the long march south. But that's the last thing on the penguins' mind on this sunny day!

FIORDLAND PENGUIN

DID YOU KNOW?

Bob is an emperor penguin. This is just one of many species, or different kinds, of penguin. On this page you can see five other kinds. Which do you think is the smallest penguin? Yes, it's the Little penguin!

BOB

EMPEROR PENGUIN AND CHICK

ADÉLIE PENGUIN

JACKASS PENGUIN

LITTLE PENGUIN

CHINSTRAP PENGUIN

ARE THERE OTHER FLIGHTLESS BIRDS AS WELL AS PENGUINS?

Yes, there are quite a few flightless species, and you can see some of them on this page. Ostriches live in Africa, the similar emu in Australia, and the Darwin's rhea in South America. The cassowary is from New Guinea. The other three birds live in New Zealand, and the kiwi is the country's national symbol.

CASSOWARY

EMU

DARWIN'S RHEA
(NANDU)

OSTRICH

TAKAHE

KAKAPO

KIWI

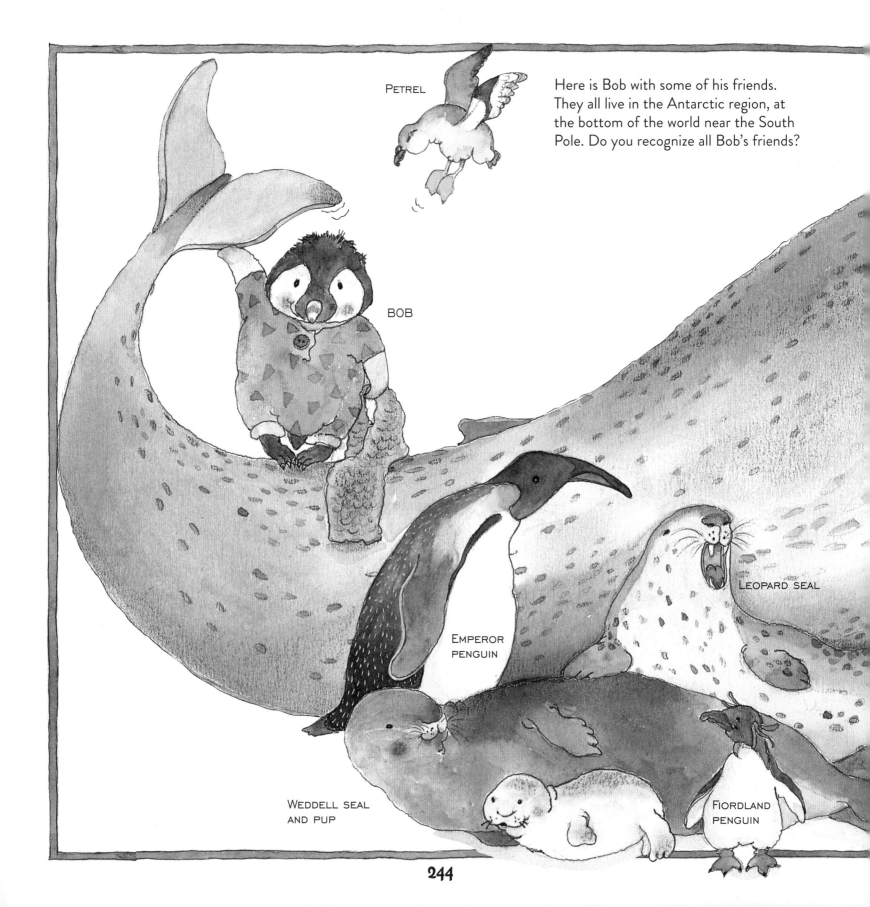

PETREL

Here is Bob with some of his friends.
They all live in the Antarctic region, at
the bottom of the world near the South
Pole. Do you recognize all Bob's friends?

BOB

LEOPARD SEAL

EMPEROR
PENGUIN

WEDDELL SEAL
AND PUP

FIORDLAND
PENGUIN

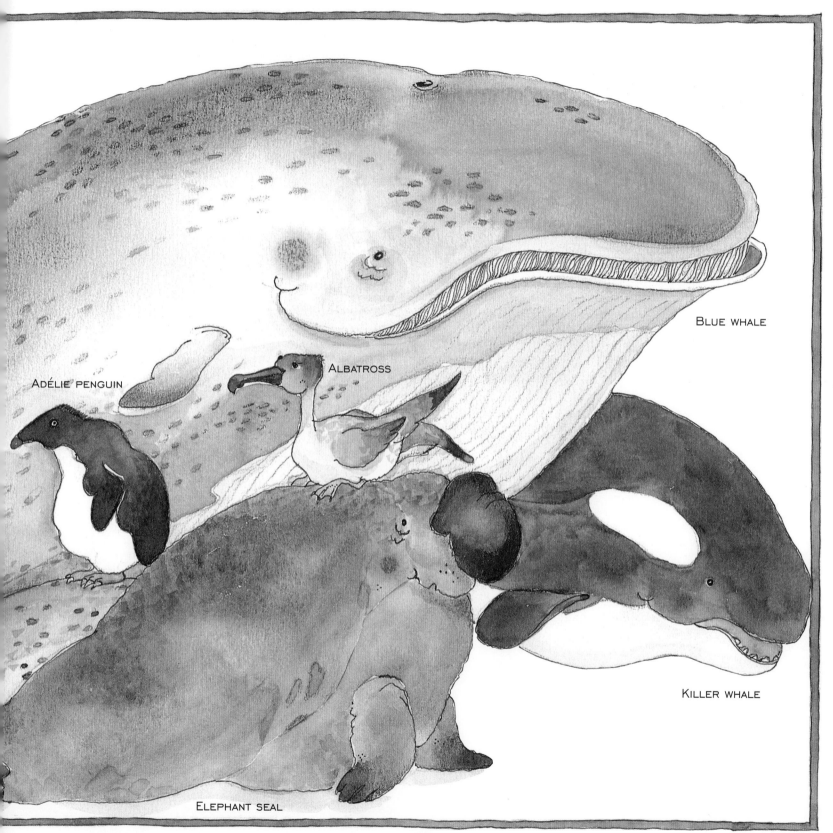

Blue whale

Albatross

Adélie penguin

Killer whale

Elephant seal

Quiz

DO YOU REMEMBER THESE
ANIMALS FROM THE STORIES?
FOLLOW THE LINES TO FIND
THEIR NAMES.

Brown bear

Eagle owl

Pangolin

Chimpanzee

Dormouse

Marmot

Adélie penguin

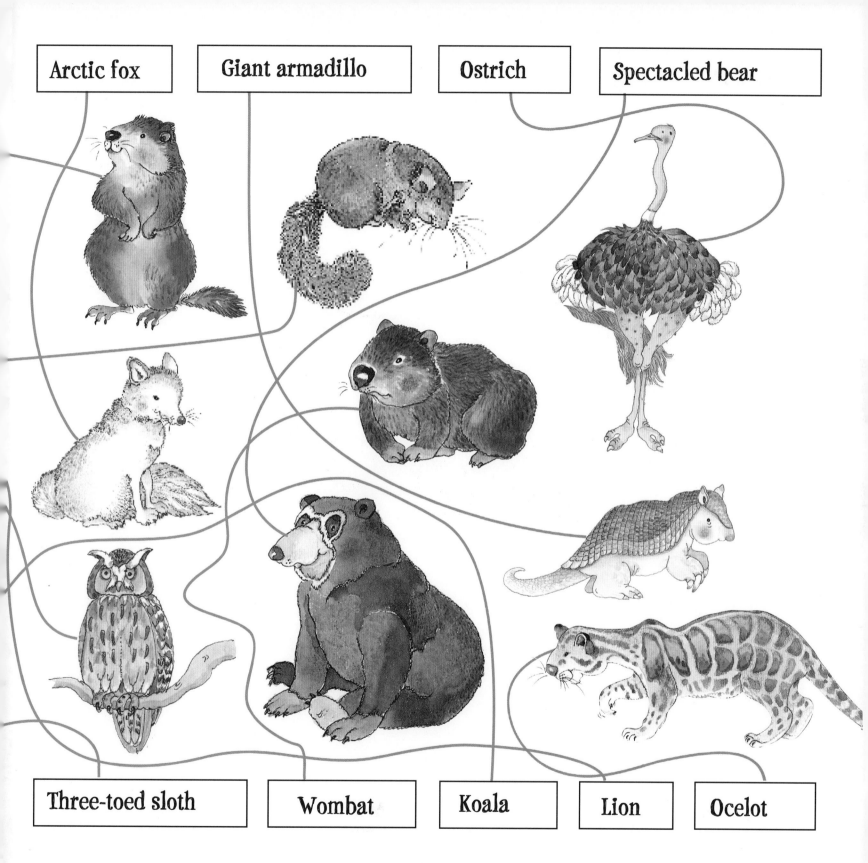

Arctic fox

Giant armadillo

Ostrich

Spectacled bear

Three-toed sloth

Wombat

Koala

Lion

Ocelot

247